Little Passports®
A GLOBAL ADVENTURE

A Musical
Mishap

Written by Megan E. Bryant

Illustrated by Carrie English

5

Sam & Sofia's Scooter Stories

First paperback edition printed in 2020 by Little Passports, Inc.
Copyright © 2020 Little Passports
All rights reserved
Manufactured in China
10 9 8 7 6 5 4 3

Little Passports, Inc.
27 Maiden Lane, Suite 400, San Francisco, CA 94108
www.littlepassports.com
ISBN: 978-1-953148-04-9

Contents

1 The Visitor.....................................1

2 The Search 7

3 The Smallest Clue 21

4 The Stage Door 28

5 Don't Get Caught!.........................33

6 The Docks.....................................42

7 The Underwater World.................48

8 Camel Café 56

9 One More Clue...............................62

10 Koolewong Lane 69

11 Click-Click!....................................77

12 The Sticky Reacher-Outer 82

13 Sparkle..90

14 In the Spotlight 94

1

The Visitor

Sam and Sofia opened the ladder's long legs with a **th-clunk!**

Sofia held out a banner of star-covered Australian flags. "You want to do the honors?" she asked.

Sam smiled and shook his head. "It was your idea," he said. "Go for it."

Sofia flashed him a grin and stepped up onto the ladder as Sam steadied the legs.

Near the top rung, Sofia leaned forward and attached one end

of the banner to the wall. She then scrambled back down, moved the ladder a few feet with Sam's help, and climbed back up to attach the other end of the banner.

Click-click!

"Are you taking pictures?" Sofia asked with a laugh. Of course, she already knew the answer. Sam never went anywhere without one of his cameras. He took photos of everything. All their neighbors on Compass Court knew that Sam had a good eye for taking pictures.

"Just capturing all the progress we've made," Sam said. "Say cheese!"

"Cheese and crackers!" Sofia joked.

Just then, Sofia's dad, Papai Luiz, poked his head into the room, followed by Sam's Aunt Charlie.

"I thought I heard that creaky, clunky old ladder," he said.

"Wow!" Aunt Charlie said. "I never thought this little room could look like this. I'm sure Kirra will feel right at home when she arrives."

Sofia grinned. "Thanks," she said. "We couldn't have done it without you two."

Compass Court had been buzzing with excitement

AN EVENING
OF MUSIC
~ with ~
SPECIAL GUEST
KIRRA!
COMPASS COMMUNITY
CENTER THEATER
at 7:00 p.m.
see front office for tickets

for weeks. Kirra, a famous musician from Australia, was touring the United States, and her very first stop was the stage at Compass Community Center!

Sam and Sofia had prepared for Kirra's arrival by making posters and selling tickets. But they were most proud of how they'd fixed up the room next to the community theatre. Once used for dusty old storage, it had been transformed. Now there were comfy chairs with lots of pillows, a table covered in colorful mosaic tiles, and a wall of photos from Australia.

"So, tell me about the special person who inspired this redecoration," Aunt Charlie said.

Sofia's eyes brightened. "Her name is Kirra," she said, "and she's one of the best musicians in Australia! She plays *in . . . in . . . indigenous*

Australian instruments." Sofia glanced at Papai. "Did I say it right?"

He nodded. "*Perfeitamente*," he replied.

"Huh?" Sam asked.

Sofia smiled at her dad. "*Perfeitamente* means 'perfectly' in Portuguese," she said.

"I know that one," Sam said. "What does *indigenous* mean?"

"Oh! Indigenous people," Sofia said, "are the people who originally lived in a certain place before others moved there from different countries. Kirra plays indigenous instruments that were created in Australia, like the didgeridoo and clapsticks and—"

"Clapsticks?" Aunt Charlie asked. "I've never heard of those before."

"The didgeridoo gets all the attention," Sofia said with a giggle.

"Do you think Kirra will bring the clapsticks with her?" Sam asked.

"Of course!" a voice said from the doorway. "It wouldn't be much of a concert without them."

Everyone turned around to see who had spoken. Sofia stepped out of the huddle, her heart sparkling with excitement.

2

The Search

Kirra stood in the doorway, beaming at everyone in the room. Her hair, the color of copper, shone as brightly as a new penny. Kirra's jewel-toned silk scarf shimmered against her skin.

Sofia's mother, Mama Lyla, and a tall man with blond hair helped Kirra move a cart piled high with luggage and instrument cases into the room. Sofia noticed right away that each case was marked with a special design: the letter K inside a wreath of narrow leaves.

"G'day," Kirra said with a nod of her head. "I'm Kirra. This is Geoff. He plays percussion with me."

"And you all know me," Mama Lyla joked with a little wave that made everyone laugh.

"Welcome to Compass Community Center," Papai Luiz said.

"You're really here!" said Sam. He immediately held up his camera and took a picture.

Click-click!

"I'm really here," Kirra said. She reached her arms behind her back and stretched. "What a long flight," she said. "Worth it, though. I love seeing new places!"

"I know how that feels," Sofia said.

Kirra smiled. "This is quite a place you've got here. I'm thrilled to launch the North American leg of my tour at Compass Community Center!"

"We'd be delighted to give you a proper tour," Mama Lyla said. "But would you like to rest a bit first?"

"Sofia and Sam decorated this room just for you," Papai Luiz added.

"Did you really?" Kirra asked in delight. "I adore it!"

"We printed lots of pictures from Australia," Sofia said, pointing at the wall.

"I have a whole wall of pictures like that in my studio," Kirra said.

"My favorite is that koala hanging in a eucalyptus tree," Sofia said.

"Look at that wee *koolewong*," Kirra cooed. "That surely reminds me of home. There's a eucalyptus grove out back of my house that's

10

fairly teeming with them."

"*Koolewong*?" Sofia repeated. "I thought they're called koalas."

Kirra smiled knowingly. "We've got a right lot of names for them in Australia," she said, ticking them off on her fingers. "*Koolewong* is the name we used when  I was a kid. Then there's *koala*, of course, and *kula*, *colo*, and *coola*, for a start."

"Why do they have so many names?" Sam asked.

"Funny thing," Kirra said. "Long ago, my ancestors noticed that koalas never seemed to need water. So each nation gave the animal a name that meant 'no water' in its language."

"Nation?" Sam asked.

"That's what we call each group of indigenous Australians," Kirra explained. She glanced at another photo. "Ahh, look at that. The crown jewel of Sydney—the Sydney Opera House! It's not just for opera,  you know. All kinds of performances happen there. It was an honor to play there on my tour."

"You performed there?" Sofia asked as she stared at the photo. The Sydney Opera House was unlike any building she'd ever seen before, with swooping white sail-shaped structures jutting into the sky. "There must have been a *million* people in the audience."

Kirra threw back her head and laughed. "Not quite a million," she said. "But even the smallest space at the Sydney Opera House is wonderful. Speaking of performing," she added. "Want to see my instruments?"

"A sneak peek?" Sam asked.

"And maybe a private concert," Kirra added

with a wink. She bustled over to the luggage cart and lifted an enormous case from it. Geoff hurried over to help. Together, they unzipped the case to reveal Kirra's didgeridoo. The long wooden instrument was nearly as tall as Sofia, with beautiful white designs carved into the polished wood.

"Whoa," Sam said.

"That's what I was thinking," Papai Luiz said. "What a beautiful instrument. Is it heavy?"

"Not so bad," Kirra said. "It's hollow inside, you know. The didgeridoo is the oldest wind instrument in the world."

"How do you play it?" Sam asked.

"Like this," Kirra said, bringing the end to her mouth. She took a deep breath and began to play the didgeridoo. Its low sound was beautiful and haunting. It seemed to rattle the whole room. Sofia could even feel it vibrating in her chest.

Kirra turned back to the cart. Her hand hovered in the air, moving from one case to another. Then she turned back to Sam and Sofia. "Why don't you choose the next one? Perhaps the gum leaves? Or the clapsticks?"

Sofia and Sam exchanged a glance. It was hard to choose.

"Surprise us," Sofia finally said.

"The gum leaves it is!" Kirra announced. She started rummaging around the luggage cart. As she searched, the smile on her face slowly faded to a frown of concern.

"Geoff?" she asked. "Have you seen the gum-leaf case?"

"Well, not since . . ." he began. Then Geoff scrunched up his face as he tried to remember.

"I don't think it's here!" Kirra exclaimed, her voice tight with worry. "I've searched all these bags and I don't see it anywhere!"

"Let's all look," Mama Lyla said. "We can retrace our steps in case it fell off the cart."

 "Look," Geoff said, holding up his phone. "I have a picture of it."

As soon as she glanced at the photo, Sofia could understand why Kirra was so upset. The gum-leaf case was a beautiful container with the same wreath symbol that decorated Kirra's other instrument cases.

"It's very distinctive," Mama Lyla said. "I'm sure we'll find it."

The group searched the entire community center from top to bottom and front to back. Soon there was no way to deny the truth any longer: the gum-leaf case was gone.

"I hope it's not lost completely," Kirra said, shaking her head. "My mum and I made it together back when I was starting out. Maybe we left it somewhere in Australia?" she asked, turning to Geoff.

"I'm sure it will turn up," Geoff said.

"Come with me," Mama Lyla said as she wrapped her arm around Kirra's shoulders. "You must be hungry after your journey. We'll get you some food to eat and then you can rest."

"We'll keep looking. I'm sure there's something we can do to help," Aunt Charlie said.

Sofia blinked. She knew Aunt Charlie was speaking to the whole group, but at the same time, it felt like her words were meant for Sofia and Sam alone. Just like that, Sofia knew what they needed to do—and from the look on Sam's face, he felt the same way.

Geoff started making calls as Mama Lyla led Kirra to the kitchen. No one seemed to notice Sam and Sofia slip out of the room.

"Are you thinking what I'm thinking?" Sam

asked as they ran toward his house.

"If you're thinking we need to search for Kirra's case in Australia, then the answer is yes!" Sofia replied.

"Great minds think alike," Sam said.

It only took a quick run down Compass Court to reach Sam's house and slip into the garage. With Aunt Charlie at the community center, her garage-turned-lab was unusually dim and quiet.

Sofia crossed the room and pulled a tarp off something large standing in the corner.

Swoosh!

The fabric fell away to reveal Aunt Charlie's most amazing invention: a globe-trotting scooter. It was a brilliant shade of candy-apple red that always seemed to shimmer, even in the lowest light. The scooter had room for two passengers, a secret compartment for Sam and Sofia to stash their stuff, and a high tech touch screen instead of a control panel.

When Sam first brought Sofia to the garage to show her the invention, neither one of them could have guessed the red scooter would end up transporting them around the world!

"I hope we can find Kirra's gum-leaf case," Sofia said. "Australia's a big country."

"And continent!" Sam added with a grin.

Sofia reached into her pocket and pulled out a small notebook. With the stub of a pencil, she began to make a list.

"What are you writing?" Sam asked.

"The places Kirra mentioned back at Compass Community Center," she explained. "There was her house, with the eucalyptus trees out back—"

"And the Sydney Opera House," Sam added.

"Right! And we know that Kirra definitely had the case when she performed there," Sofia said. "That should be our first stop."

"To the Opera House!" Sam said.

Sofia climbed onto the scooter with Sam

right behind her. She tapped the touch screen, which glimmered as a spinning globe appeared. Familiar words flashed across the screen.

Sofia entered the words *SYDNEY OPERA HOUSE, AUSTRALIA.*

"Ready?" she asked.

"Ready!" Sam replied.

Sofia pressed the green button on the screen.

"*Vamos!*" she cried in excitement.

Whiz . . . Zoom . . . FOOP!

3

The Smallest Clue

Every time the red scooter transported Sofia and Sam to a new place, Sofia couldn't help but close her eyes against the blazing light that surrounded them. It was a reflex. After a few moments, though, she could feel the rumbling engine slowing down and could sense the light beginning to fade away. When she opened her eyes and blinked, she gasped.

The light from the scooter had been replaced by bright sunshine. They were in Australia!

Cars, trucks, and motorcycles ruffled Sofia's hair as they zoomed by. In the other direction, a brisk breeze blew in off the ocean, scenting the air with salt and seaweed. Sofia was about to ask Sam if they were near the Great Barrier Reef when she saw, for the very first time, the Sydney Opera House.

It was even more majestic in person than in pictures. Tall structures shaped like sails, or maybe seashells, swooped into the brilliant blue sky. The building was covered with gleaming windows that sparkled in the sunlight. Below the opera house, the waters of Sydney Harbor lapped at the pier.

"Wow," Sofia said in awe.

Next to her, Sam didn't respond—at least, not with words.

Click-click! Click-click!

The snapping of his camera told Sofia that he was just as captivated by the impressive building as she was.

"It's ginormous!" Sofia said.

"Let's check it out," Sam finally replied.

They parked the red scooter in a nearby passageway, then ran across the vast pavilion, taking the steps two at a time.

As they approached the Sydney Opera House, they realized how big it really was. Like Kirra had told them, it offered a lot more than opera. There were posters for all kinds of events, from rock concerts to plays to comedy shows. There were even restaurants and cafés where people were enjoying refreshments. As they admired the posters, Sofia grabbed a map of the Sydney Opera House from a nearby display.

Sofia opened the pamphlet and turned to Sam with a worried look on her face.

"The gum-leaf case is so small, and the Sydney Opera House is so big," she said. "How will we ever find it—even if it is here?"

"You're right," he began. "There's no way we could search the whole place. That would take hours. Days! Maybe even weeks!"

"We definitely don't have weeks," Sofia said. "We need to think of a plan."

"A strategy," Sam agreed.

"What did Kirra say again?" Sam asked, drumming his fingers on his knee as he tried to remember. " 'Even the smallest spaces at the Sydney Opera House are wonderful?' "

Sofia scanned the map. "Some spaces look smaller than others, but it's hard to tell. Does the map show how many seats there are in each room?"

For a moment, the two friends were silent as

they studied the map. Sofia traced her finger along the shape of the Sydney Opera House.

"This one has a couple hundred seats," Sam said. "The Utzon Room. It looks the smallest."

"If Kirra said 'smallest,' " Sofia said, "She must have played the Utzon Room! *Vamos!*"

The friends followed the map across the courtyard. When they reached the stairs leading up to the main level of the Sydney Opera House, though, Sofia grabbed Sam's elbow.

"No, not the main entrance," she said.

"How else do we get in?" Sam asked.

4

The Stage Door

Sofia pointed at a label on the map: *Stage Door.* "That's where performers like Kirra would enter," she said.

"Perfect" Sam said. "It's like a secret entrance!"

Sofia lifted her finger from the map and

pointed beyond the stairs. "And it's right over there!"

As they approached the stage door, Sofia spotted a crew of people carrying several items into the building from the back of a big truck. She felt a flicker of doubt. Surely *someone* would notice them sneaking in—and then what would they do?

"There are too many people," Sofia said. "But maybe if we—"

"Hey, you two!" a voice called behind them.

Sofia and Sam turned to see a group of crew members carrying a big crate toward the stage door. The tallest of the group was looking straight at them.

"Yes?" Sofia asked timidly.

The tall man smiled. "Will you grab that door for us?" he asked politely.

Sam could barely hide his laughter.

"Yes. Yes, of course!" Sofia said.

She scurried to the stage door and held it open as the crew maneuvered the box inside. After they'd cleared the door, Sofia and Sam looked at each other, scurried inside after them, and ducked down a side hallway. And just like that, Sam and Sofia were inside the Sydney Opera House!

The backstage area was like a maze of shadowy tunnels. Sofia felt like a wombat in an underground burrow. The pipes snaking overhead were like roots hanging down against the rough brick of the windowless walls.

They followed the map, using the screen of Sam's camera to light the way, and when they

came to another door, Sofia looked up. "This is it—the Utzon Room," she whispered. "The smallest performance space in the Sydney Opera House."

Sam pressed his ear against the door. "I don't hear anything," he said in a low voice. "But it might be soundproofed."

"We don't want to rush in," Sofia said. "What if there's a concert happening right now?"

Sam nodded, then pressed his finger to his lips. Slowly, slowly, *slowly*, he turned the handle and pushed the door open, just a fraction of an inch at a time. Meanwhile, Sofia moved forward as the door opened, peeking through the itty-bitty crack until, at last, she could confidently say—

"It's empty!"

Sam and Sofia stepped into the Utzon Room and closed the door behind them. As they stood in front of a beautiful tapestry, Sofia could picture Kirra at the front of the room, surrounded by 200 people as she played her indigenous instruments.

She shook her head. "Focus," she said, almost to herself. "Let's split up. I'll search for the gum-leaf case here, and you can search the nearest dressing room."

Sam nodded in agreement. "Perfect," he replied. "I'll meet you back here in 10 minutes. And whatever you do—"

"Don't get caught!" they said at the same time.

5

Don't Get Caught!

As Sam disappeared into the hall, Sofia began to search the performance space. It wasn't a huge room, but even the small gum-leaf case could easily get misplaced here. As she looked under and around each chair and music stand, a growing worry tugged at her heart. What if she was in the wrong room altogether?

Sofia's thoughts broke off abruptly as she spotted something. A cream-colored rectangle of paper was partially concealed by one of the chairs, but the bright sunshine streaming through the windows made it almost glow. She hurried across the room, picked up the paper, and laughed with relief.

Sofia recognized the wreath with the letter K in the middle right away. It was a program from Kirra's performance!

"So she *was* here," Sofia said to herself.

"But *you* shouldn't be here," someone said from the doorway.

Sofia glanced up in alarm and saw Sam—and a security guard—standing across from her.

34

She scrambled to her feet. "I—I—I—" she stammered.

"Calm yourself, young lady," the guard said. He wasn't smiling, but it almost seemed as if his eyes were twinkling. "Your friend here told me all about your little excursion."

Sofia's forehead wrinkled in confusion. It didn't seem like Sam to tell a total stranger about their search for Kirra's gum-leaf case. It would cause so many questions about the scooter and where they'd come from. "But—"

"I know it's your dream to be on this stage—" the guard began.

Sofia blinked in confusion "My dream . . . ?"

Sam caught her eye and Sofia took a breath. "Ohhhh, oh yes," she said, playing along. "I just wanted to see what it would be like inside the Utzon Room."

"If you work hard enough, you'll find your way onto the stage," the guard said. "I'm sure of it. Until then, though, you'll have to take a scheduled tour like everybody else. I can't allow you to wander about back here, willy-nilly! Now, if you'll allow me to escort you out—"

Great cover story, Sam, Sofia thought, smiling to herself. She jammed her hand—still holding the program—into her pocket. She couldn't wait to show it to Sam.

Then she had an idea.

"You must get to see a lot of concerts, huh?" she asked the guard. "Did you catch Kirra's show? We're big fans!"

"That was a great concert," the guard said with a grin.

"You saw it?" Sam asked. "Really?"

"Yes, yes. A very nice woman, Kirra," the guard said. "So nice to the crew."

"Do you have a Lost and Found?" Sofia continued. "I wonder if any of the performers have ever left anything behind. I would be so upset if I left one of my instruments here," she added.

"It's the audience that leaves things behind," he replied in a confidential tone. "The performers usually have people looking after them. Besides, we do a clean sweep of each space before the next performer arrives. If something was forgotten, we'd find it fast."

"That makes sense," Sofia said as they reached the stage door.

"Keep working hard, and maybe one day I'll see you perform on one of our stages," the guard said. Then he turned back and closed the door, leaving Sam and Sofia outside.

"Nice job with that cover story!" Sofia said.

"I had to think of something," Sam said. "I didn't want him—"

"—asking about the scooter," Sofia finished. "Any clues in the dressing room?" she asked.

"Nothing," Sam said, shaking his head. "I don't

think we've been looking in the right place."

Sofia smiled. "Maybe this will convince you."

She pulled the program from her pocket and handed it to Sam, watching him as he read it. The moment he realized that the program was from Kirra's show in the Utzon Room, a broad grin crossed his face.

"Well, it's not the gum-leaf case," he said, "but who knew I'd be so happy to see a crumpled piece of paper?!"

"I know what you mean," Sofia said. "It feels good to know we're making progress! But from what the guard told us, I don't think the case is here." She  pulled out her notebook and offered it to Sam. "Want to cross off the Sydney Opera House?"

Sam, still staring at the program, didn't answer.

"Sam?" Sofia prompted him. "Earth to Sam!"

At last, Sam looked up, his eyes bright with excitement. "Sofia!" he exclaimed. "Did you see this?"

Sam tapped on the program and Sofia stared at the small print under his fingers. It took her a moment to realize what she was reading. "It's—" she began.

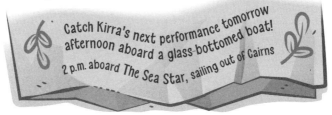

Catch Kirra's next performance tomorrow afternoon aboard a glass-bottomed boat! 2 p.m. aboard The Sea Star, sailing out of Cairns

"An ad for Kirra's next performance!" Sam yelped with excitement. "Check it out—the day after the Utzon Room, she played on a glass-bottomed boat over the Great Barrier Reef. The Sea Star, sailing out of Cairns!"

"This is incredible!" Sofia cried. "Sam! Do you

know what this means?"

"We're going to see the Great Barrier Reef?" Sam asked, clutching his camera.

"Well, yes," Sofia replied with a giggle. "And hopefully that boat is where we'll find Kirra's case, too!"

With that, they took off running for the red scooter. There was no time to lose!

Whiz . . . Zoom . . . FOOP!

☑ The Sydney Opera House

☐ The Sea Star!

6

The Docks

When they arrived in Cairns on the scooter, ocean spray cooled Sofia's cheeks. She could hear gulls flying overhead, their squawking cries echoing on the sea breeze.

Sofia squinted in the sunlight and held her

hand over her eyes. The sprawling city of Cairns stretched out in front of her. At the edge of the city were the docks, jutting out into the crystal clear ocean water.

Sofia looked out at the boats floating near the docks. It was amazing to think that, somewhere nearby under the surface of the water, the Great Barrier Reef was teeming with ocean life.

"The docks look like their own city," Sofia said. "But instead of buildings, they're filled with boats."

"Dozens of boats," Sam said. "Hundreds of boats! How are we going to find the *Sea Star*?"

Sofia scrunched up her nose, deep in concentration, as she tried to answer Sam's question. There were sailboats and fishing boats, motorboats and yachts. There was even a giant cruise ship, as big as a floating hotel. It was going to be tricky to find one particular boat among all the others.

"I know!" Sofia exclaimed, snapping her fingers. "Tickets!"

"Huh?" Sam asked.

"People buy tickets to ride boats like the *Sea Star*," she explained. "Instead of searching for the boat out *there*—" She paused to fling her arm out toward the docks. "—we can find the ticket booth over *here*. *Vamos!*"

Sam and Sofia parked the scooter and roamed around the docks, searching every building, shed, and kiosk for a sign about the glass-bottomed boat where Kirra had performed. Finally, they spotted a kiosk with a large model of a starfish perched on top.

"Starfish . . . *sea star!*" Sofia exclaimed.

"Do they mean the same thing?" Sam asked.

"I have a feeling they do," she replied.

Inside the kiosk, a teenage boy was stocking guides to the Great Barrier Reef in a display. His name tag read "Mason."

"Excuse me," Sofia said. "Can you tell us where to find a boat called the *Sea Star*?"

"I surely can," Mason replied. "The ship's just out yonder. You may still be able to catch a glimpse of her."

"Catch a glimpse?" Sam repeated.

Mason nodded. "She set sail about fifteen minutes ago."

"Oh, no!" Sofia cried. They had just missed it.

"Don't worry," Mason said. "The *Sea Star* will be back in a few hours. It takes people out to the reef all day. The coral doesn't grow right on the shore here. You'd have to go to Fitzroy Island for that. We do have some conservation displays along the docks, though. They give you a sneak peek. Or you could buy tickets for tomorrow's tour."

Tomorrow will be too late, Sofia thought.

"Do you have a Lost and Found?" Sam asked.

"Oh, now I see why you're so upset," Mason said knowingly. He reached under the counter and pulled out a box. "We keep everything that gets left behind in this box, where it's safe and sound until someone comes searching for it. So, what are you missing?"

Sam and Sofia eagerly peered into the box.

7

The Underwater World

Sofia carefully rummaged through the items in the Lost and Found box. There wasn't much inside it: a tube of lip balm, a seashell bracelet, a couple Australian coins.

"Is this everything?" Sam asked.

"Afraid so," Mason said. "Don't see what you're looking for?"

Sofia shook her head. "It's not here."

"Sorry, mate," Mason said.

"Thanks anyway," Sofia said.

Sam and Sofia left the kiosk and wandered onto the dock, which had glass portholes along the walkway. They were like windows into an underwater world.

"Check it out!" Sofia exclaimed.

"Whoa," Sam said. "I've heard of glass-bottomed boats, but never glass-bottomed docks!"

"This must be one of the displays Mason was talking about," Sofia said, "It's more than a sneak peek. It's amazing!"

Delicate coral structures spiraled up from the ocean floor as wispy strands of seaweed waved in the current. Different groups of tropical fish in a rainbow of colors darted through the coral.

The fish moved so fast that Sofia didn't dare blink. She didn't want to miss seeing a single one.

"All that coral is alive, you know," Sam said in a hushed voice. "It's part of the largest coral reef in the entire world."

"It's beautiful," Sofia said. As she watched the fish swim through the crystal clear water, her disappointment about reaching a dead end in Cairns started to wash away. Within a few minutes, she was ready to come up with a new plan. Sofia stood up and straightened her shoulders.

"What now?" Sam asked as he scrambled to his feet.

"Think, think, think," Sofia said, tapping her temple. "I guess the case could still be on the boat, but can we wait around for hours to find out?"

Sam shook his head. "We're going to run out

of time before Kirra's performance starts back home," he replied.

"Think, think, think," Sofia repeated.

As they neared the kiosk, Sofia noticed that Mason was replacing posters and fliers at a nearby bulletin board. He noticed Sam and Sofia, too. "Oi! Come here," he called out. "I've got something for you."

Sofia and Sam followed Mason back to the kiosk.

"I'm sorry you missed the boat," Mason was saying. "I thought this might make you feel better. Take your pick." He picked up a wooden box that rattled as it moved.

Sam and Sofia leaned forward curiously to look inside. The box was filled with seashells and sea glass!

"We can have one?" Sofia asked.

Mason nodded and smiled. "Consider it a souvenir of your visit to Cairns," he replied.

"These are hard to come by, too," he added. "The reefs are protected. We only keep shells that are safely collected and sold."

"Wow," Sam whispered, leaning closer.

Sofia picked a cream-colored shell that was speckled with brown spots. It took Sam longer to choose, but at last he selected one that was smooth and bright white.

"Thanks so much for the shells," Sam said. "Can we take a selfie with you?"

"Of course, mate," Mason replied. The three friends crowded together and grinned for the camera.

Click-click!

"Now, if you'll excuse me," Mason said, "I've got to swap out the weekly adverts."

Sofia watched Mason return to the bulletin board. Then her eyes grew wide. "Wait!" she cried as she ran over to the board.

Sofia heard Sam gasp behind her as she pointed at what she'd seen: a poster with Kirra's signature wreath of leaves— and Mason was about to tear it down!

Mason turned around in surprise. "What's the matter, then?" he asked.

"Can we have that poster?" Sofia asked urgently.

"Fine by me," Mason said with a shrug. "It was headed for the rubbish bin anyway. That concert's over and done with."

But for Sam and Sofia, the poster wasn't trash.

It was another clue! Beneath Kirra's signature wreath icon were the words *The Camel Café in Alice Springs welcomes Kirra!*

"*Last chance to see Kirra on her Australian tour,*" Sofia read from the poster's headline. "Sam! Do you know what this means? This is where she played after the *Sea Star.*"

"And if this was her last performance in Australia, this is probably where she lost the gum-leaf case!" Sam added. "So I guess this means we're going to . . ." He paused to read the poster. "Camel Café in Alice Springs!"

Sam stashed the poster in his messenger bag as the pair raced back to the scooter. Within moments of climbing aboard, Sofia had typed their destination into the touch screen.

"Camel Café, here we come!" Sofia said.

Whiz . . . Zoom . . . FOOP!

8

Camel Café

The red scooter brought them to a side street in a small town. Beyond the buildings, the landscape was dry and dusty, red and rocky. Scrubby plants had popped up here and there, thriving despite the intense heat.

Sam and Sofia found some shade and parked the red scooter before venturing into town.

"I didn't know there were mountains in the outback," Sam said. He focused his camera on the peaks in the distance.

Click-click!

"You'd get a better view of the MacDonnell Ranges if you got a bit closer," a woman told them.

Sam and Sofia turned toward her.

"Sorry—what did you say?" Sam asked.

The woman wiped her hands on her apron and gestured to the mountains. "The MacDonnell Ranges," she replied. "You'll want to see them up close, I reckon. They've got hiking trails and swimming holes—a lot to explore, if exploring's a thing you like."

Do we ever, Sofia thought, smiling to herself. "Thank you!" she said to the woman. "If we have time, we'll definitely check them out."

"Here for the camel races, then?" asked the woman. She smiled proudly. "Alice Springs is famous for them."

"No," Sam said. "We're looking for, let's see . . ." He pulled the poster from his messenger bag and glanced at the headline. "Camel Café."

"Why didn't you say so?" the woman said, chuckling.

Sam and Sofia gave each other the same confused look.

"Well, you've already found it," the woman continued, gesturing to the door behind her. "Camel Café is my place! You can call me Tilda."

"So this—this is where Kirra performed?" Sofia asked in excitement.

Tilda's face lit up. "Fans of Kirra's, are you?"

she asked. "So am I! Come in, then. Any fan of Kirra is a friend of mine."

Sofia didn't want to bombard the woman with questions, but she couldn't help herself. "Do you know—did Kirra leave anything here?" she asked urgently. "One of her instruments, maybe? Or a case for an instrument?"

"One with the shape of a wreath on it?" Tilda asked.

"Yes!" Sofia said, her excitement growing.

"With the letter K inside it?" Tilda continued.

"Yes!" Sam said.

Sofia held her breath. Was Tilda about to reveal the very thing that had brought them all the way to Australia?

Tilda threw back her head and laughed. "My goodness," she finally said. "If Kirra had left something here, I'd have sent it on to her, I promise you. No, she didn't leave anything behind. But her logo is lovely, isn't it?"

Sofia felt all the hope drain out of her. She couldn't hide it—and neither could Sam. *Another wild goose chase*, she thought glumly. And even worse, now they didn't know where else to look.

9

One More Clue

Tilda's laughter faded as she saw Sofia and Sam's disappointment.

"Dearies, you look like you've gotten some awful news," she said. "Come, now, it can't be that bad. Have a seat. I'll get you something cold to drink."

Until that moment, Sofia hadn't realized how thirsty she was. She licked her dry lips.

Tilda led them inside, and a few minutes later, she bustled out of the kitchen carrying a tray with two glass bottles and a plate.

"Ginger and lemon soft drinks," she announced, placing the bottles on the table with a clink. "Nice and chilled and just about guaranteed to quench your thirst."

"Thank you," Sam and Sofia said together.

Sofia took a long sip of the ginger soda. "Wow," she said. "That's sweet and spicy at the same time!"

"The lemon one is so good," Sam said.

"Switch?" Sofia suggested.

"Switch," Sam agreed as they exchanged

frosty-cold bottles.

"And this is what we call fairy bread," the woman said, placing the plate in the middle of the table. It was piled high with buttered bread that was topped with sugary sprinkles in every color.

"Mmm," Sofia said. "That looks delicious!"

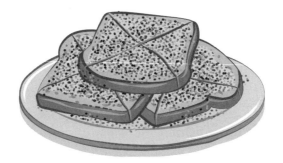

"Now, since it's so important to you, I'll go into the back and see if Kirra left something behind I missed," Tilda continued. "Don't get your hopes too high, though. I don't want you to be disappointed."

"Thanks for checking," Sam said gratefully.

"And for all the treats," Sofia added.

Sam and Sofia sat back in the cool, dim room of the Camel Café. It was nice to sit for a while, after racing all around Australia.

"We'll rest for a little bit, and then we'll figure out what to do next," Sofia said, and Sam nodded.

Sofia let her mind wander as she glanced around at the decorations in the Camel Café. She couldn't imagine going back home without the gum-leaf case. Right now, they didn't have any more leads, but surely there were more places in Australia for them to search.

Just then, Tilda returned from the back of the café.

"Sorry, loves," she said, shaking her head. "Just as I suspected, Kirra didn't leave anything behind before she went back to Wagga Wagga. But I wouldn't want to send you away empty-handed."

She held out a paper bag. Inside, it was crammed with all kinds of different candies:

ginger chews, striped peppermints, licorice strips, fizzy gumballs, and chocolate-covered honeycomb.

"Sweets for the sweet," Tilda told them.

Sofia smiled at Tilda's gift. She had the same warm energy as Kirra. "Thank you so much," Sofia replied. "Um . . . what's Wagga Wagga?"

"That's the town where Kirra lives," Tilda said.

"Oh! Sure. Of course," Sofia said. "I knew that."

"She's been in that same darling house all the years I've known her," said Tilda.

"With all the eucalyptus trees, right?" Sam asked.

"And the koalas out back?" Sofia added.

"Oh, yes," Tilda said with a chuckle. "It's called Koolewong Lane for a reason."

Sofia grinned at Sam, and he grinned back. Just like that, they had one more clue to follow! Maybe Kirra had returned home before taking her flight to Compass Court. The gum-leaf case could be somewhere at her house!

Sofia picked up the bag of candy. It was heavier than she expected. Tilda had filled it to the brim. Sofia didn't want to leave without giving something to Tilda in return. She began to search her pockets and found a button, seven paperclips, two bolts . . .

And the speckled shell from Mason.

Sam and I don't need two *souvenirs,* Sofia thought as a smile spread across her face. She turned to Tilda.

"Sam and I want to give you this," she said as she held out the shell.

Tilda's whole face lit up. "What a beauty!" she cried. "I don't make it to the coast very much, so this is a right treat for me. Thank you both!"

"Selfie?" Sam asked, holding up his camera.

Tilda smiled. "It would be my pleasure," she replied.

Click-click!

Sofia and Sam said goodbye to Tilda and hurried back to the red scooter. The sun had shifted, making it glitter even more brightly. Sofia was so eager to type in their final destination in Australia that her fingers were practically twitching.

"Here we go," Sofia said as she tapped the green button.

Koolewong Lane
Wagga Wagga, Australia

Whiz . . . Zoom . . . FOOP!

10

Koolewong Lane

When they arrived in Wagga Wagga, Sofia and Sam jumped off the scooter. The glowing sunset bathed the quiet road in warm pink light.

"Do you think that's where Kirra lives?" Sofia

asked, gesturing to a quaint white cottage. Beyond the low fence that surrounded it were endless grassy fields, and just over the cottage's roof, Sofia could see rounded treetops.

"That must be the eucalyptus grove!" she continued, pointing at the trees.

"Then we're in the right place," Sam said. "Let's explore."

There was an emptiness about the cottage, but as the friends approached, they could see signs of Kirra everywhere. A wind chime made of sticks and beads, similar to Kirra's necklaces, rattled in the breeze; the rocking chair on the porch was covered in a patchwork quilt that reminded Sofia of Kirra's scarf; and most Kirra of all—

"Check it out," Sam said as he peeked in the garage window.

"Another lab?" Sofia joked.

"Not exactly," Sam replied. "It looks like a

music studio!"

"Wow," Sofia said. Then—she wasn't quite sure why—she tried to turn the doorknob. And to her astonishment, the door swung right open.

"Hello?" Sofia called out. "Is anyone here?"

For several long moments, she waited for an answer, but none came.

"Let's go inside," she said to Sam.

Sam hesitated in the doorway. "Are you sure we should?" he asked in a low voice. "What if we get in trouble?"

Sofia scrunched up her face. "I mean, we're here to help," she said. "We'll just take a quick look. We have to see if the case is here."

"Okay," Sam agreed, still sounding a little nervous.

There were all kinds of musical instruments in Kirra's studio, including drums and mandolins and even a harp. It was perfectly organized, without even a single page of sheet music out of place. It didn't take long for Sam and Sofia to realize the gum-leaf case wasn't in the studio.

Sofia didn't want Sam to see how disappointed she was. She walked over to one of the walls, which was covered with photos and artwork. There were beautiful indigenous Australian paintings, patterned with hundreds of dots that formed images of lizards and landscapes. There were also dozens of photographs featuring wildlife from Australia, from colorful clownfish darting through the coral reef to a kangaroo leaping through the outback.

There was also a photo of Kirra and Geoff standing in front of the Sydney Opera House smiling wide with their instruments in front of them. Below the photo was a handwritten note.

"Sam," Sofia said urgently. "Look!"

"What is it?" he asked, walking over.

Sofia pointed at the photo of the Sydney Opera House and the note beneath.

"So she *did* come home before leaving for Compass Court," Sam said. "How else would she have put this photo up?"

"Exactly!" Sofia said.

"The case has to be here!"

"But where?" Sofia asked.

Next to the picture of Kirra and Geoff was a photo of a koala with a big brown splotch on her head—and this photo also had a note under it.

Sparkle the Koala
loves her gum leaves

Sofia tilted her head to the side and read the caption again. It said "gum leaves," but the leaves, and the trees, looked awfully familiar.

"Sam, what's that koala eating?" she asked, pointing at the photo.

"Eucalyptus leaves," he replied.

"But the caption says it's eating *gum* leaves," Sofia said. "Do you know what this means?"

"Spell it out for me," Sam said, looking confused.

"If *eucalyptus* leaves and *gum* leaves are the same thing, then all those eucalyptus trees out back—"

"Are also gum trees!" Sam was so excited, he couldn't help interrupting. "Just like there are lots of names for koalas, maybe there are lots of names for eucalyptus trees too."

"If we go into the grove out back, we can get Kirra some new gum leaves!" Sofia exclaimed.

Sam looked at the photo again. "All this time,"

he said, "we've been in here looking for gum leaves when there are tons of them growing just outside." He shook his head. "But Kirra will still be without her case."

"What if . . . ." Sofia began.

"What if what?" Sam asked.

11

Click-Click!

"**I**f you were a koala," Sofia said, "what would you do with a gum-leaf case?"

Sam looked thoughtful. "I'd try to open it, I guess," he said. "To eat—hold on. What are you thinking?"

"Maybe a *koala* took the gum-leaf case!" Sofia exclaimed. "Think about it—if it smelled like gum leaves, and the koalas basically live right in Kirra's backyard . . ."

"What an incredible theory!" Sam said. "And if I were a koala with a case full of gum leaves, I might climb up into a tree, where I'd feel safe. Let's go to the eucalyptus grove before we lose the light."

"Koalas are nocturnal," Sofia said in a low voice while they walked around Kirra's house. "I remember reading that they're really active at dawn and dusk."

"So, right about now," Sam said as they reached the grove.

Sofia nodded, then stepped quietly into the grove. She didn't want to startle any koalas that were just waking up from a long nap. Sofia peered up into the trees, trying to spot something . . . anything. The gray-green leaves made a shadowy canopy, and Sofia had trouble seeing anything beyond the lowest branches. She sighed.

"I can't see very well either," Sam said, guessing her thoughts.

Suddenly, his eyes brightened. "I have an idea!" he said as he reached for his camera.

"What are you thinking?" Sofia asked.

"I'm going to photograph each tree," he said. "Then we can brighten the screen and zoom in on the image. We'll get a much better look at each tree—and anything that might be in it."

"Genius!" Sofia said.

Sam lifted the camera to his face, focusing it on the nearest tree in the grove.

Click-click!

Sofia stared over Sam's shoulder at the camera's screen. She saw bark, branches, leaves—and nothing else.

"Nothing," she said, shaking her head.

"Nothing," Sam replied. "Onto the next tree."

Click-click!

Once more, Sofia and Sam eagerly searched the camera screen.

"*Nada*," Sofia said, using the Portuguese word her father had taught her.

Sam glanced up from the camera screen. "*Nada*," he agreed. "Next."

Click-click!

When Sam zoomed in on the photo, Sofia sucked in her breath. This time, she was sure she could see something sparkle in a crook of the tree.

"Sam!" she said urgently, pointing at the screen. "Is that what I think it is?"

12

The Sticky Reacher-Outer

Sam held up the camera. The image was blurry but unmistakable: the gum-leaf case, sparkling in the crook of a branch.

"We did it!" Sofia shrieked with glee. Then,

remembering the sleepy koalas, she clapped her hands over her mouth. "Oops! I mean, *we did it!*" she repeated in a whisper.

"We found Kirra's gum-leaf case!" Sam marveled. "Now the only thing we have to do is figure out how to get it down."

"No problem," Sofia replied. "I love climbing trees."

"Wait," Sam whispered, holding up his hand. "We can't disturb the koalas. They feel safe here. This is their habitat."

"We haven't even seen any koalas, though," Sofia said.

"Or have we?" Sam asked. He zoomed in on the photo again and handed the camera to Sofia. "I'm pretty sure that's a paw there—right under that clump of leaves."

Sofia looked up, wide-eyed. "You mean there's a koala in that tree—right there? The one with the gum-leaf case?"

Sam nodded. "I'm thinking your theory was correct," he told her.

Sofia reached into her pockets and dumped everything onto the ground. She sorted through the buttons, hairbands, paper clips, and rubber bands. There was her yo-yo, her pencil, her notebook, the bag of candy from Tilda—

"Aha!" Sofia exclaimed softly, shaking the bag of candy. "Now I have an idea."

"I'm listening," Sam said, eyeing the candy.

"I know you said we shouldn't climb the tree because we might disturb the koala," she began. "But what if I climbed the *other* tree? You know, the one next to it, where we *didn't* see any signs of koalas?"

"How are you going to get the case if you're in a different tree?" Sam asked.

Sofia grinned, then rummaged around in the candy bag. She pulled out a bright green gumball. "Something sticky," she said, picking up a fallen branch, "on the end of something long . . . I think I can reach."

Sam looked thoughtful. "I dunno," he said slowly. And just when Sofia thought Sam wasn't onboard, he reached into the bag and pulled out a big yellow gumball. "Mmm, lemon," he said, and he popped it into his mouth and started chewing.

Sofia smiled and popped the green gumball in her mouth. "Apple," she announced.

The friends chewed quickly in silence until Sofia's jaw got tired.

"Okay," Sam said, pulling the gum from his mouth. "Mine is really sticky." He stretched it between his fingers.

"Mine, too," Sofia replied.

They each squashed their gum onto the end of the long stick.

"The sticky reacher-outer is ready," Sofia announced. She tucked it under her arm and approached the tree.

"Be careful," Sam said, sounding a little worried. "Climb slowly, and don't get too close to any koalas."

"I got this," Sofia said confidently.

Then, like she had done so many times with other trees in Compass Court, she started to climb. It was getting darker by the minute, but Sofia could've climbed a tree while blindfolded. One hand at a time, up, and up, and up . . .

She soon reached a sturdy branch that was about the same height as the nook where they'd spotted the case in the opposite tree. She perched on it, steadying herself with one hand, and then she spotted the case! It was as beautiful as she expected.

"Okay," she whispered to herself. "Here goes nothing."

With one arm wrapped around the eucalyptus tree's trunk, Sofia held out the stick. She reached

as far as she could—she reached as far as she dared—the gummy end of the stick inching closer and closer to the gum-leaf case in the other tree . . .

"Just . . . about . . . there . . ." she murmured.

With one last reach, Sofia touched the stick to the gum-leaf case—and pulled it out of the tree!

"Got it!" she whisper-shouted in triumph. "Here, Sam . . . catch!"

Then she dropped the sticky reacher-outer.

Sofia heard Sam's soft voice call "I have it!" from below.

She was about to climb back down when she noticed that the leaves were rustling in the other tree. She froze, every muscle of her body tense.

Then Sofia heard something faint, but unmistakable: the sound of someone—or something—chewing.

13

Sparkle

With her heart racing, Sofia glanced over—and spotted a wild koala! It lounged against the tree trunk, lazily dropping eucalyptus leaves into its mouth. Its brown eyes shone in the twilight as it looked at Sofia.

"Sparkle?" she whispered. "Is that you?"

Of course, the koala didn't respond. But Sofia was pretty sure she knew the answer. The brown spot on the koala's forehead—which, now that Sofia thought about it, almost looked like a star—told Sofia everything she needed to know.

"Sorry we had to take back the case," Sofia said. "I hope you enjoy your dinner—or . . . is it your breakfast?"

"Sofia?" Sam called from the ground. It was so dark now that she could barely see him.

"I'll be right down," she said.

"Wait!" he replied. "The case is empty. Looks like *somebody* ate all of Kirra's gum leaves. Can you pick some while you're up there?"

"You got it," Sofia said. She grabbed a handful of leaves, then climbed back down the tree as carefully as she could.

Sam was waiting for her, holding open the gum-leaf case. Sofia tucked the leaves in and closed it. The beaded design shimmered even in the dim light of the gum tree grove.

A grin spread across her face as she thought about how happy Kirra would be to see it.

"Guess what?" she asked, pointing at the tree. "Sparkle's up there."

"Really?" asked Sam.

Sofia nodded. "I'm sure of it. I wish you could've seen her. She's beautiful. So fluffy and cuddly-looking."

A smile spread across Sam's face as he grabbed his camera. He focused on the tree and—

Click-click!

Then Sam pulled up the picture and zoomed in until they could both see Sparkle on one of the branches. "There she is!" he announced.

"She looks like she's ready to go back to sleep," Sofia said, muffling her laughter.

"Then we'd better get out of here," Sam said.

The two friends tiptoed out of the grove. Back

at the red scooter, Sofia typed Sam's address into the touch screen. She shut her eyes, anticipating the blinding light.

Whiz . . . Zoom . . . FOOP!

14

In the Spotlight

Suddenly, there they were: right back in the corner of Aunt Charlie's lab, where their adventure had started.

"Hey, not bad," Sam said as he checked the battery. "We still have twenty percent power!"

"We'd better charge the scooter for next time," Sofia said. They didn't know when—or where—they'd go, but Sofia had a funny feeling that there'd be another trip in the very near future.

As Sofia plugged in the charger, Sam pulled the gum-leaf box from his messenger bag. Then they ran to Compass Community Center as fast as they could.

The halls of the community center were unusually quiet.

"What time is it?" Sofia asked breathlessly. "Are we late?"

"I don't know," Sam replied. "Run faster!"

At the entrance to the theatre, Sofia and Sam paused—just for a moment—to catch their breaths. Then Sofia eased open the door.

The theatre was dark, but Sam and Sofia could still see that almost every seat was filled. On stage, standing in the spotlight, Kirra seemed to glitter. Her instruments were arranged on a long table covered with a bright cloth. Geoff sat to the side with his percussion instruments.

"Before we begin, I have a brief announcement," Kirra was saying. "Our order of songs will be a wee bit different from what appears in your program. Unfortunately, the gum leaves I planned to play—"

"Are right here!" Sofia yelled out, surprising even herself. Every head in the audience turned to look at her. Kirra peered into the seats from the stage, squinting under the lights.

Sam and Sofia ran down the long aisle. By the time they reached the stage, Sam was holding

the gum-leaf case high. Kirra recognized it at once.

She gasped and pressed her hands to her heart. "You found it! My gum-leaf case!"

She opened the case and pulled out the gum leaves Sofia had picked.

"They're just as I packed them!" Kirra said happily.

Sam and Sofia looked at each other and exchanged a secret smile.

Kirra turned back to the audience. "Strike what I just said," she announced. "Thanks to my two new friends here, we will begin with a freestyle jam, as listed in your programs."

Sam and Sofia stepped away from the stage.

"Where are you going?" Kirra asked them with a warm smile. "We've got music to play!"

"Us?" Sofia asked, and there was some laughter from the crowd.

"Yes, you two," Kirra said. "Come on up here for a song!"

Sofia and Sam exchanged a glance and

walked slowly on stage. Sofia saw Aunt Charlie sitting in the audience next to Papai Luiz and Mama Lyla. It was hard to see past the bright stage lights, but Sofia was sure she saw Aunt Charlie give them a wink.

"Here you go, mate," Geoff told Sam as he handed him a large sheet of metal. "I think you'll be a natural on the wobble board."

Geoff demonstrated the wobble board for Sam—and the audience—at the same time. Moving it back and forth made an otherworldly sound that echoed across the stage.

Meanwhile, Kirra opened a wooden case and removed two clapsticks. The polished wood gleamed, highlighting the intricate shapes and symbols carved into the sticks.

"They're beautiful," Sofia breathed.

"My grandfather carved these clapsticks," Kirra said proudly as she held them up for the audience to see. "When I play them it's like I can still hear him playing them as the firelight flickered and sparks danced up to the stars."

She began to tap out a fast-paced beat, using the narrow and wide end of the clapsticks to keep rhythm. When she rubbed them together, the clapsticks whispered *whshhh, whshhh, whshhh*. Kirra chanted words that Sofia had never heard before. For a moment, Sofia could imagine that she was sitting around that fire, too, listening to Kirra's grandfather play.

Then Kirra smiled as she held the clapsticks out to Sofia. "Want to try?" she asked.

"Me?" Sofia gasped. "Play your grandfather's precious clapsticks?"

"Of course," Kirra replied. "I can't imagine anything that would have made him happier."

Sofia's heart swelled with happiness, too, as she began to tap a rhythm with the clapsticks. Sam played the wobble board while Geoff shook a pair of seed rattles. Kirra pressed a gum leaf to her mouth, making high-pitched notes trill up and down the scale.

Each sound was so distinctly unique, but they came together to make a song that was unforgettable.

Sofia smiled at Sam from across the stage.

From the Sydney Opera House to Camel Café, they'd visited many unique performance spaces that day, but none were quite like Compass Community Center.

Sofia looked out at her family and friends in the crowd. She couldn't think of any better place to share the stage with Kirra.

The End

Australian Slang

- Ace! - Awesome! / Excellent!

- Arvo - Afternoon

- Barbie - Barbecue

- G'day! - Good day! / Hello!

- Good on'ya! - Good for you! / Well done!

- Gum leaves - Eucalyptus leaves

- Mozzie - Mosquito

- Port - Suitcase

- Prezzy - Present / Gift

- Roo - Kangaroo

- Sunnies - Sunglasses

- Ta - Thank you

- Too Right! - Definitely!

Australian Terms for Koala

- Koolewong

- Kula

- Colo

- Coola

Portuguese Terms

- Nada - Nothing

- Papai - Dad

- Vamos! - Let's go!

Sofia and Sam's Snippets

Australia isn't just a country. It's also one of the world's seven continents. That makes Australia the only place on the entire planet that's both a country and a continent.

AUSTRALIA

Canberra
(national capital)

← Australian flag

Sydney is the largest city in Australia. The world-famous Sydney Opera House is located there. It has about 1,000 rooms! Every year, about two million people enjoy performances at the Sydney Opera House.

The Great Barrier Reef is a network of living coral reefs off the coast of Australia. The reefs provide a habitat for millions of sea creatures.

There are more than 10,000 beaches throughout Australia! Some are popular tourist attractions often full of visitors, while others are private or even deserted.

Favorite ocean activities in Australia include surfing, snorkeling, and scuba diving to see beautiful tropical fish.

Kangaroo →

There are many **marsupials** living throughout Australia. Female marsupials have pouches on their bellies where they can carry their babies until they are more grown. Kangaroos, koalas, possums, and wombats are all marsupials.

Koalas have sharp claws that help them climb trees. Their favorite food is eucalyptus (gum) leaves.

Eucalyptus has a strong scent, like the menthol in some types of cough medicine. Koalas eat so much eucalyptus that some say they smell like cough drops!

In Australia, there are more kangaroos than people. There are kangaroo crossing signs along the roads to remind drivers to watch out for kangaroos.

Didgeridoo

The didgeridoo was invented by indigenous Australians, perhaps more than 40,000 years ago. It may be the world's oldest instrument!

The first didgeridoos were made of wood, but today they can be made of many different materials, including glass, leather, and even cactus.

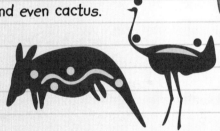

The first people to live in Australia are called indigenous Australians. Signs of early Australian civilization date back more than 50,000 years, making indigenous Australians the oldest known human society.

There are more than 100,000 rock art sites throughout Australia, where people can see artwork created by indigenous Australians over the course of thousands of years.

Fairy Bread Recipe

Ingredients:

- [ ] 3 slices white bread
- [ ] 1 stick butter (softened)
- [ ] Sprinkles, colored sugar, candy
  confetti, or a mixture of toppings

Details:

Active time: 10 minutes
Total time: 10 minutes
Yield: 6 servings
(2 triangles per person)

Fairy bread is a favorite treat in Australia. It has a special ingredient that Australians call "hundreds and thousands." In other places, people call them sprinkles or jimmies. These sweet toppings are so tiny that it's easy to see how the name "hundreds and thousands" stuck.

Fairy bread is often served at birthday parties in Australia, but you don't have to wait until your birthday to try some!

Instructions:

1. Cut the crusts off the slices of bread using a butter knife. Then cut each slice diagonally into two triangles.

2. Use the butter knife to spread about half a tablespoon of softened butter on each triangle. Make sure to use enough butter so the sprinkles will stick.

3. Add a generous layer of sprinkles to each piece of fairy bread. Enjoy with a glass of milk!

Try this!

- Use cookie cutters to cut each piece of bread into a fun shape.

- Use different colors of sprinkles to create patterns and designs on the bread. Try stripes, shapes, or a swirl.

- Flavor the butter with jam, syrup, or cinnamon sugar.

- Toast the bread first for a toasty-warm version.

Keep your adventure going with a Little Passports science subscription!

Solve real-world mysteries with fun, hands-on activities.

Fun activities, for kids of all ages, come to life with exciting, action-packed experiments. Create an erupting volcano, launch your very own catapult, and propel an air-powered rocket!

LittlePassports.com